TRANSFORMERS
RISE OF THE BEASTS

Mission at the Museum

Adapted by Natalie Shaw

Based on the screenplay written by
Joby Harold and Darnell Metayer & Josh Peters and Erich Hoeber & Jon Hoeber

Illustrated by Guido Guidi

PARAMOUNT PICTURES and SKYDANCE PRESENT IN ASSOCIATION WITH HASBRO and NEW REPUBLIC PICTURES a di BONAVENTURA PICTURES PRODUCTION A TOM DeSANTO/DON MURPHY PRODUCTION a BAY FILMS PRODUCTION
"TRANSFORMERS: RISE OF THE BEASTS" ANTHONY RAMOS DOMINIQUE FISHBACK MUSIC BY JONGNIC BONTEMPS COSTUME DESIGNER CIARA WHALEY EDITED BY JOEL NEGRON, ACE WILLIAM GOLDENBERG, ACE BRETT M. REED STUART LEVY, ACE
PRODUCTION DESIGNER SEAN HAWORTH DIRECTOR OF PHOTOGRAPHY ENRIQUE CHEDIAK, ASC EXECUTIVE PRODUCERS STEVEN SPIELBERG BRIAN GOLDNER DAVID ELLISON DANA GOLDBERG DON GRANGER BRIAN OLIVER BRADLEY J. FISCHER VALERII AN
PRODUCED BY DON MURPHY & TOM DeSANTO LORENZO di BONAVENTURA MICHAEL BAY MARK VAHRADIAN DUNCAN HENDERSON BASED ON HASBRO'S TRANSFORMERS' ACTION FIGURES
STORY BY JOBY HAROLD SCREENPLAY BY JOBY HAROLD and DARNELL METAYER & JOSH PETERS and ERICH HOEBER & JON HOEBER DIRECTED BY STEVEN CAPLE JR.
SKYDANCE BAYFILMS NEWREPUBLIC di BONAVENTURA pictures Dolby Atmos
#Transformers #RiseOfTheBeasts TransformersMovie.com @TransformersMovie @Transformers

Ready-to-Read

Simon Sp
New York   London   Toron

SIMON SPOTLIGHT
An imprint of Simon & Schuster Children's Publishing Division
1230 Avenue of the Americas, New York, New York 10020
This Simon Spotlight edition May 2023
For information about special discounts for bulk purchases,
please contact Simon & Schuster Special Sales at 1-866-506-1949 or
business@simonandschuster.com.
Manufactured in the United States of America 0523 LAK
10 9 8 7 6 5 4 3
ISBN 978-1-6659-2189-3 (hc)
ISBN 978-1-6659-2188-6 (pbk)
ISBN 978-1-6659-2190-9 (ebook)

This is Noah.
He lives with his family
in Brooklyn.
His brother, Kris, is sick.

Kris's arm is hurting.
"You have to tell me
these things," Noah says.

Noah needs money
to pay for doctors.
He thinks a car will help.

But it is Mirage,
a Transformers robot!

At the museum,
a researcher named Elena
is doing a test
on a statue of a falcon.
The statue crumbles!

Inside the statue she finds
part of the Transwarp Key.
Scourge, a Terrorcon, is looking
for the two parts of that key
so he can rule the world!

A signal shoots
out of the key.
Now the Transformers
robots know where it is.
They need to get the key
to keep it from Scourge.

Mirage asks Noah for help.
Since he is human,
he will blend in at a museum!
If he succeeds, Noah can
sell Mirage for money,
so he can help his brother.

Scourge is coming
for the key too.
He makes the power
go out!

Noah runs toward the museum.

Elena sees that Noah
is trying to get the key.
She will not let him.
She does not realize
that he is trying to help.

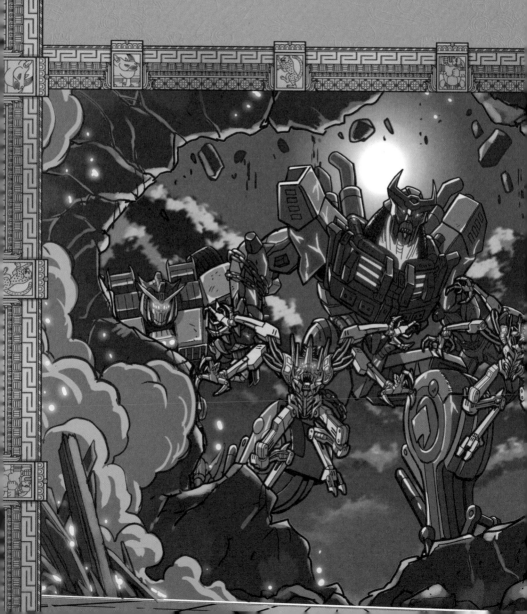

Then Scourge blasts open
the wall of the museum.
He and his Sweeps try
to get the key.
The Sweeps work for
Scourge.

Outside, the Autobots arrive.
They fight the Terrorcons.

"Run!" Elena tells Noah.
The Sweeps chase them!

Noah and Elena try to
drive away.
Nightbird stops them!

Mirage tries to help,
but Nightbird takes the key.

The Autobots fight Scourge.
Bumblebee sees that
Optimus Prime is in trouble.

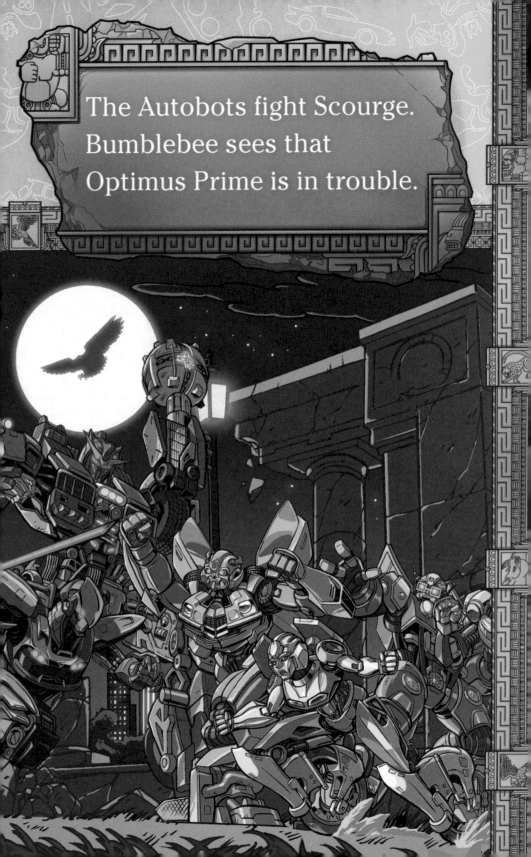

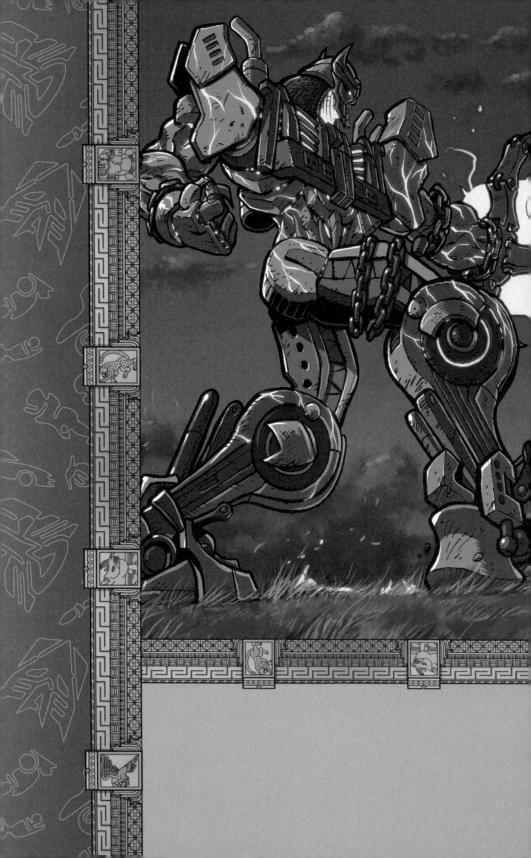

Scourge is attacking
Optimus Prime!
Bumblebee rams into
Scourge but gets hurt.

The Autobots are losing the battle.

Then Airazor flies in
and blasts fire.
Scourge fights back.

Suddenly they hear sirens.
Scourge and the Terrorcons
escape with the key!

Airazor says to Optimus Prime,
"Come with me. I can help you."

Together they will
try to find the other half
of the Transwarp Key.
They must keep Scourge
from ruling the world!